Scoop
and the Bake

Illustrations by Pulsar and Jorge Santillan

EGMONT

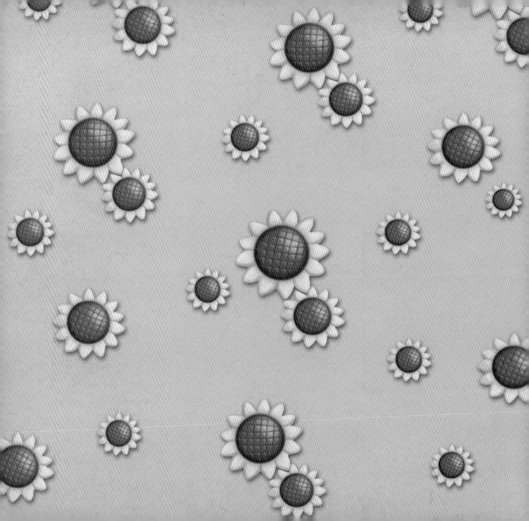

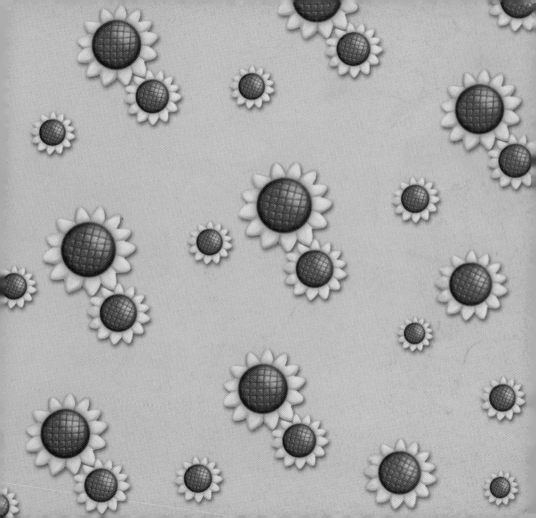

EGMONT

We bring stories to life

First published in Great Britain 2008
This edition published in 2010
by Egmont UK Limited,
239 Kensington High Street, London W8 6SA
Endpapers and introductory illustrations by Craig Cameron.

HiT entertainment

ISBN 978 1 4052 4108 3

1 3 5 7 9 10 8 6 4 2

Printed in Malaysia

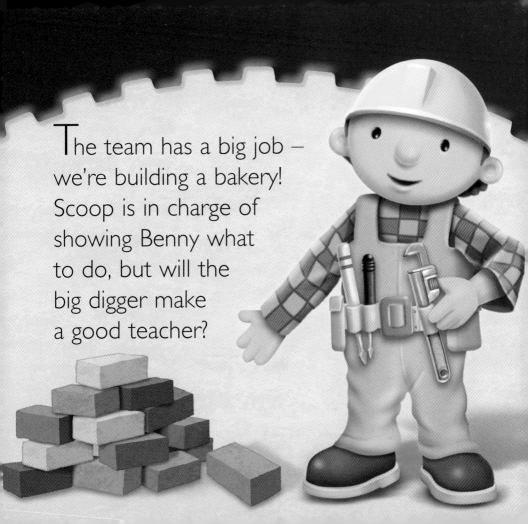

The team has a big job – we're building a bakery! Scoop is in charge of showing Benny what to do, but will the big digger make a good teacher?

One morning in the New Yard, Bob was checking he had all he needed in Travis' trailer. Dizzy, Scoop and Lofty wondered what he was up to.

"This is a flat-packed bakery — it comes in pieces!" said Bob. "We're going to put it together for Mr Sabatini, by the river."

"Coooool!" said Scoop.

"And," said Bob, "there's a surprise for you when we get there, Scoop!"

Bob and the machines made their way to the riverbank. Scoop was very excited. "So where's my surprise, Bob?" he asked.

At that moment, Benny rolled out from behind a bush. "Hi, Big Banana!" he laughed.

Scoop jumped. So that was his surprise!

"Scoop," said Bob, "we thought it would be a good idea if Benny joined you on this job and learned a few tips."

Scoop looked confused. "So, you need a digger to teach a digger?"

Bob smiled. "Who better to teach Benny than the biggest and best digger I know?"

Scoop felt happy. Then he whispered to Bob, "Are you sure I can do it?"

"Of course you can!" said Bob. "Now, let's get this lot unloaded. Can we build it?"

"Yes, we can!" cheered the machines. "Er, yeah . . . I think so," added Lofty.

Bob marked out the foundations, while Scoop told Benny what to do.

Suddenly, Spud appeared. "Ooh, what's going on here?" he asked.

"I'm teaching Benny how to make the foundations for Mr Sabatini's bakery," said Scoop, proudly.

Spud rubbed his tummy. "A bakery? That means yummy bread. I love bread, I do . . . can I help too, Bob?"

Bob laughed. "Sorry, Spud, I think we've got all the help we need today," he said.

Spud looked very sorry for himself.

Bob's next job was to collect the bakery's oven with Lofty and Travis.

"It's a clever oven, heated by burning these special briquettes," said Bob. "And we make the briquettes from pressed sunflower stalks with this machine. Look!"

Bob showed them all how it worked before setting off to fetch the oven.

When Bob had gone, Spud pleaded with Scoop to let him help. "Please! I'll do anything!"

So Scoop said that Spud could make the briquettes.

"Great idea!" smiled Spud. He was looking forward to trying some tasty bread, and skipped off with the briquette machine.

Meanwhile, Scoop and Benny began to dig the bakery's foundations.

"OK, Benny, make sure you dig inside the area marked by Bob!" said Scoop.

Before long, the digging was done and Dizzy filled the area with concrete.

"What's next, Scoop?" asked Benny eagerly.

Scoop wasn't sure, so Dizzy said they should wait for Bob.

Benny looked disappointed. "But you can do anything, can't you, Scoop?"

"Well …" Scoop said, looking flustered, "we could put up the framework."

Dizzy was worried. "You've never done that without Bob," she warned.

But Scoop said he'd watched it being done lots of times. "And Benny's got to learn somehow!" he added.

So the two diggers got to work.

"Wow! You know your stuff!" Benny grinned, when the framework was in place. "What's next? The roof?"

"Well, I suppose we could …" said Scoop.

"We should wait for Bob!" Dizzy huffed.

Scoop didn't listen and lifted up the roof. But the framework wasn't strong enough and the roof began to wobble! Scoop hurried underneath to support it . . . but his wheels sunk into the wet concrete!

Benny and Dizzy rushed off to find help. Moments later, Bob, Lofty and Travis arrived – just in time to rescue Scoop.

"I'm sorry, Bob," cried Scoop. "All I've taught Benny is how to make mistakes!"

"Oh, Scoop," said Bob, kindly. "We all need help sometimes. And you've taught yourself a good lesson today!"

"Yes! Next time, I won't try to do things all by myself," Scoop promised.

"OK, team!" said Bob. "We've a bakery to finish! Can we build it?"

"Yes, we can!" called the machines.
"Er, yeah . . . I think so," added Lofty.

They all set to work, levelling the concrete and fixing the framework, roof and walls.

Mr and Mrs Sabatini arrived, just as the special oven was being wheeled inside.
"It's magnificent!" they said happily.
"Thank you so much, everyone!"

Just then, Bob remembered something. "We forgot to make the briquettes for the oven!" he cried.

"It's OK, I asked Spud to do it!" said Scoop.

"Phew!" smiled Bob. "What would I do without you, Scoop?"

Later, Mr Sabatini baked the very first loaf of bread. It was shaped just like Scoop!

"Ha, ha! Scoop," drooled Spud. "You're the tastiest digger in Sunflower Valley!"

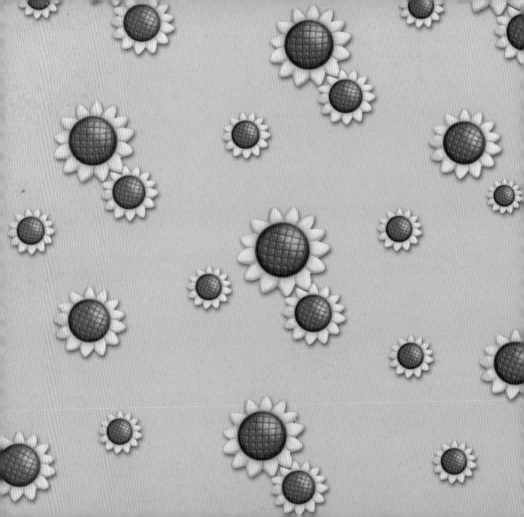

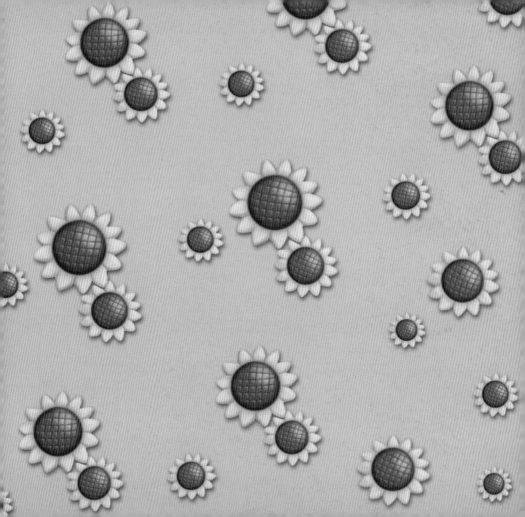